CAPTAIN RAPTOR
and the SPACE PIRATES

KEVIN O'MALLEY *and* **PATRICK O'BRIEN**

Illustrations by **PATRICK O'BRIEN**

Walker & Company ✸ New York

IN THE MISTY SKIES ABOVE THE PLANET JURASSICA, A *DARK AND SINISTER SHAPE* IS SEEN MOVING AMONG THE CLOUDS.

THE HATCH FLIES OPEN, AND A *MOB OF MISSHAPEN MUTANTS* AND *REPTILIAN CYBORGS* FLOW LIKE A RIVER OUT OF THE SHIP, SCREAMING AND SHOUTING AND WAVING THEIR LASER SWORDS.

THE CITIZENS OF JURASSICA ARE IN A *PANIC* AS THE SPACE PIRATES RAID THE IMPERIAL PALACE.

SMASHING THROUGH A HEAVY DOOR, THE RAMPAGING ROGUES FIND THE FAMOUS *JEWELS OF JURASSICA*.

WEIGHED DOWN WITH TREASURE, THE PIRATES DASH BACK INTO THEIR SHIP AND BLAST OFF, LEAVING THE PALACE IN RUINS.

"*THOSE PIRATES MUST BE STOPPED!*" ROARS THE PRESIDENT.

"BUT SIR, WHAT CAN WE DO?"

"I'LL TELL YOU WHAT WE DO. WE CALL . . ."

THE STARSHIP *MEGATOOTH* IS PREPARED FOR BATTLE.

CAPTAIN RAPTOR ASSEMBLES HIS FEARLESS CREW:

PROFESSOR ANGLEOPTEROUS: MASTER ENGINEER.

SERGEANT BRICKTHOROUS: WEAPONS SPECIALIST.

LIEUTENANT THREETOE: ACE PILOT.

"OKAY CREW, *BUCKLE UP*," SAYS CAPTAIN RAPTOR. "LET'S TEACH THOSE HOOLIGANS A LESSON THEY WON'T FORGET! *3...2...1...*"

CAPTAIN RAPTOR'S TRUSTY PILOT, LIEUTENANT THREETOE, IS AT THE CONTROLS AS THE *MEGATOOTH* *RACES THROUGH SPACE*, FOLLOWING THE *BLACKROT'S* ION TRAIL.

THROUGH THE STAR CLUSTER OF REPTILIUS 4, FAR AROUND THE PERILUS NEBULA, THE *MEGATOOTH* CHASES THE FLEEING PIRATES.

AT LAST, CAPTAIN RAPTOR SPOTS THE *BLACKROT*, DRIFTING WITHOUT POWER NEAR A SMALL, UNKNOWN MOON.

"CAPTAIN," SAYS THREETOE, "SEE THAT SMOKE? THEIR SHIP IS DAMAGED. *NOW'S OUR CHANCE! I'M GOING IN!*"

"NO, *PULL BACK*, THREETOE. *I SMELL A TRAP!*"

TOO LATE! **BLAM! BLAM! BOOM!** THE MEGATOOTH IS **BLASTED** WITH TONS OF MOLTEN LEAD.

CAPTAIN RAPTOR AND HIS CREW GO *SPINNING UNCONTROLLABLY* TOWARD THE ROCKY MOON.

COULD THIS BE *THE END* OF CAPTAIN RAPTOR?

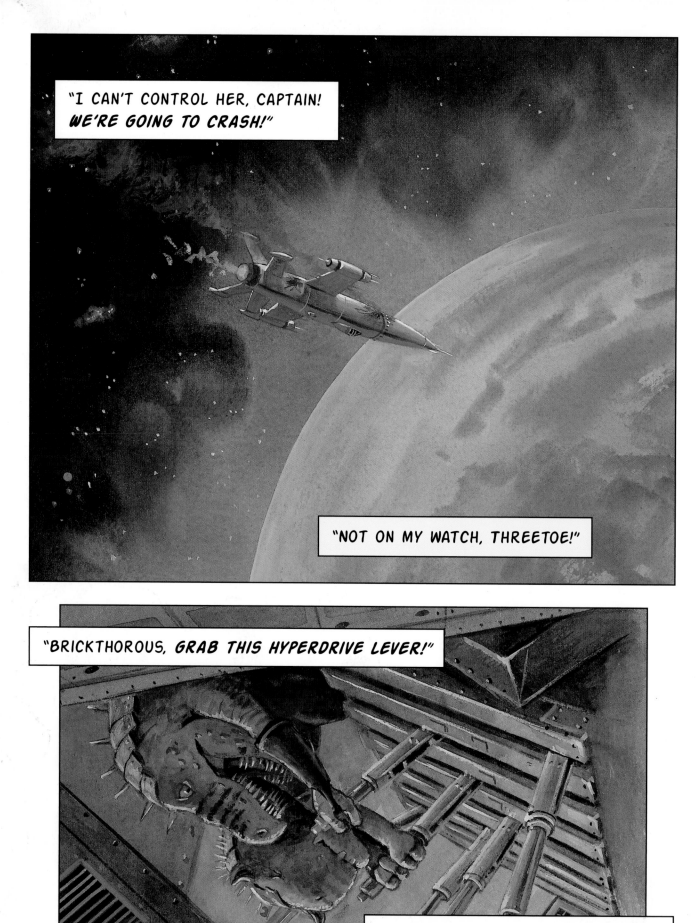

AT THE LAST MOMENT, CAPTAIN RAPTOR AND BRICKTHOROUS MANAGE TO CONTROL THE SPIN AND GET HER NOSE UP. THE *MEGATOOTH* HITS *HARD*, THEN SCRAPES AND SLIDES TO A STOP.

THE CAPTAIN AND CREW STAGGER OUT ONTO A BARREN LANDSCAPE.

"STRANGE, THIS MOON DOESN'T SHOW UP ON ANY OF MY SPACE MAPS. AND IT SEEMS TO BE COMPLETELY DESERTED."

ANGLEOPTEROUS EXAMINES THE SHIP'S ENGINES. "CAPTAIN, OUR PLUTONIC SERVOSCOPE IS SHATTERED. THERE'S NO WAY TO FIX IT—WE DON'T HAVE THE PARTS. I'M AFRAID WE'RE STUCK HERE."

"WHAT ARE YOU DOING HERE?" DEMANDS CAPTAIN RAPTOR.

"AH, SIR, I WAS JUST GETTIN' READY TA ASK *YOU* THE SAME THING."

"*I* AM CAPTAIN RAPTOR OF THE PLANET JURASSICA. NOW, WHO ARE YOU?"

"ME NAME? WHY, IT'S BLOODY BART SCALA—ER, UH—IT'S BART SCALAWAG, SIR. AND 'TWAS A BAND OF *ROTTEN PIRATES* THAT DONE IT, CAP'N. CAPTURED ME SHIP AND LEFT ME HERE, THE SCURVY DOGS. LEFT ME *MAROONED* ON THIS MISERABLE PLANET."

"BUT I SEE YER IN A SPOT OF TROUBLE. LOOKS LIKE YER SHIP'S SEEN BETTER DAYS. YA MIGHT BE NEEDIN' A BIT OF MY HANDIWORK, THEN?"

"I DOUBT IT. NOT UNLESS YOU'VE GOT A NEW PLUTONIC SERVOSCOPE UNDER THAT CAPE."

"WHY, I CAN RIG UP THAT OLD BARGE OF YERS AND HAVE HER ALL SHIPSHAPE IN NO TIME, CAP'N. BUT YOU'LL HAVE TO BE TAKIN' ME WITH YA WHEN YA BLAST OUT OF HERE."

CAPTAIN RAPTOR STARES INTO SCALAWAG'S BEADY EYES, THEN SAYS, "VERY WELL."

"PUT YER TRUST IN ME, CAP'N. YOU WON'T REGRET IT."

TRUE TO HIS WORD, SCALAWAG REPAIRS THE BROKEN SHIP.

"NOW, THREETOE," SAYS CAPTAIN RAPTOR, "*LET'S GET THIS BIRD IN THE AIR.*"

THE *MEGATOOTH* SLOWLY LIFTS OFF THE GROUND.

"CAP'N," SAYS SCALAWAG, "I RECKON THOSE RAPSCALLIONS HAVE HEADED BACK TO JURASSICA. THERE'S STILL MORE TREASURE TO BE FOUND THERE.

AND WITH YOU OUT OF THE WAY, THERE'D BE NO STOPPING THEM.

IF I WAS A PIRATE, THAT'S WHAT I'D DO.

AND MAY I SAY, SIR, THAT IF YOU WAS TO FLY RIGHT THROUGH THE PERILUS NEBULA, YOU'D GET TO JURASSICA TWICE AS FAST."

"THAT'S RISKY, SCALAWAG. MANY SHIPS HAVE GONE INTO THE NEBULA, BUT FEW HAVE COME OUT.

BUT JURASSICA NEEDS US. WE'LL HAVE TO TAKE THE CHANCE. THREETOE, *TAKE US IN.*"

THE *MEGATOOTH* ENTERS THE NEBULA, A MYSTERIOUS CLOUD OF GAS AND COSMIC DUST.

"THIS PLACE GIVES ME THE CREEPS, CAPTAIN," SAYS THREETOE.

"HOLD IT TOGETHER, MAN. YOU CAN DO THIS. STEADY ON," SAYS CAPTAIN RAPTOR.

"*LOOK OUT!*" YELLS SCALAWAG. "*HERE COMES TROUBLE!*"

ROBOKRON!

THE **GIANT ROBOTIC SPACE BEAST** CIRCLES THE **MEGATOOTH**, ITS **SPIKY JAWS** OPEN WIDE!

"TAKE THAT!" SHOUTS BRICKTHOROUS, FIRING A BLASTOCANNON. BUT THE BURST JUST **BOUNCES OFF** THE MONSTER'S METAL SKIN.

COULD *THIS* BE THE END OF CAPTAIN RAPTOR?

"**CAP'N!**" SHOUTS SCALAWAG. "I'VE TANGLED WITH THIS MONSTER BEFORE. IF YOU CAN GET TO THE ELECTRIC PANEL ON ITS NECK, YOU CAN CUT ITS POWER LINE. THAT'S **THE ONLY WAY** TO DEFEAT IT!"

CAPTAIN RAPTOR CLIMBS OUT THE HATCH, **LEAPS** ONTO THE ROBOKRON'S BACK, AND CLAMBERS UP TO ITS NECK. OPENING THE ELECTRIC PANEL, HE SEES DOZENS OF WIRES. **WHICH ONE TO CUT?**

WITH THE ROBOKRON'S TEETH SLOWLY **CRUSHING** THE MEGATOOTH, CAPTAIN RAPTOR REACHES IN AND **YANKS OUT** EVERYTHING HE SEES.

THERE'S A **SHOWER OF SPARKS**, AND THEN A **HUGE ELECTRIC JOLT** HURTLES HIM BACK ONTO THE MEGATOOTH.

THE ROBOKRON GOES LIMP AND BEGINS TO FALL JUST AS CAPTAIN RAPTOR **DIVES** INTO THE *MEGATOOTH'S* HATCH.

"*STEP ON IT, THREETOE!* LET'S SEE WHAT THIS SHIP CAN DO!"

THE *MEGATOOTH* **ZOOMS** OUT FROM BELOW THE FALLING MONSTER, THEN **SPEEDS** BACK THROUGH SPACE TO JURASSICA.

ARRIVING IN THE SKIES ABOVE JURASSICA, THE *MEGATOOTH* LIES IN WAIT.

BRICKTHOROUS CHARGES UP THE BLASTOCANNONS. "*READY FOR BATTLE*, CAPTAIN," HE REPORTS.

SOON, THE PIRATE SHIP EMERGES FROM THE MISTS.

"*FIRE!*" YELLS CAPTAIN RAPTOR. *THE BATTLE IS ON!*

CAPTAIN RAPTOR TURNS TO SHOUT AN ORDER AT SCALAWAG, BUT NO ONE IS THERE. "NOW WHERE'D THAT RASCAL GO?"

JUST THEN HE SEES THE *MEGATOOTH'S* SHUTTLE CRAFT LEAVING THE SHIP, WITH *BART SCALAWAG* GRINNING AT THE CONTROLS.

SCALAWAG TURNS ON THE RADIO COMMUNICATOR AND SHOUTS AT THE PIRATES, "*LET ME THROUGH, YA SCURVY DOGS!* BLOODY BART SCALAWAG HAS RETURNED! AND YOU'LL NOT GET RID O' ME THIS TIME!"

THROUGH A *HAIL OF CANNON FIRE*, THE SHUTTLE CRAFT MAKES ITS WAY TO THE PIRATE SHIP AND GLIDES INSIDE.

"WE CAN'T TAKE MUCH MORE OF THIS," SHOUTS THREETOE. "THE BLACKROT'S TOO BIG FOR US. WE'RE SHOT FULL OF HOLES!"

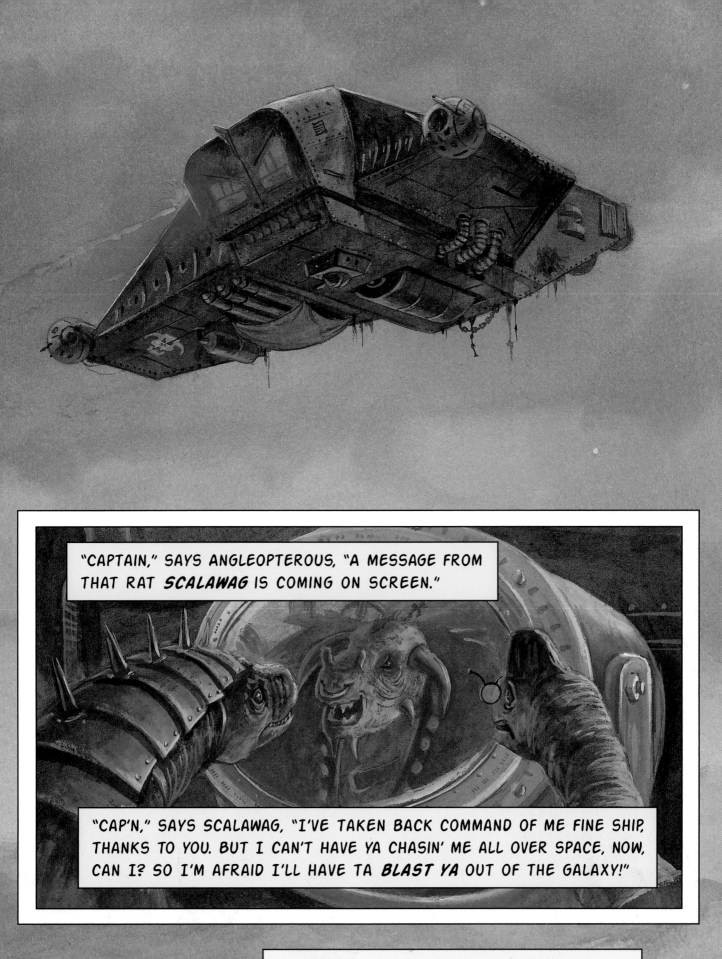

"CAPTAIN," SAYS ANGLEOPTEROUS, "A MESSAGE FROM THAT RAT *SCALAWAG* IS COMING ON SCREEN."

"CAP'N," SAYS SCALAWAG, "I'VE TAKEN BACK COMMAND OF ME FINE SHIP, THANKS TO YOU. BUT I CAN'T HAVE YA CHASIN' ME ALL OVER SPACE, NOW, CAN I? SO I'M AFRAID I'LL HAVE TA *BLAST YA* OUT OF THE GALAXY!"

IS *THIS* THE END OF CAPTAIN RAPTOR?

KA-BOOM

THE BACK OF THE *BLACKROT* IS TAKEN OFF BY THE EXPLOSION. THE SHIP *SPIRALS* DOWN TO THE PLANET BELOW.

THE PIRATES TUMBLE OUT, DAZED AND DEFEATED. TONS OF TREASURE SPILL ONTO THE GROUND.

THE DINOSAURS OF JURASSICA CAN REST EASY NOW. CAPTAIN RAPTOR AND HIS FEARLESS CREW HAVE *SAVED THE DAY* AGAIN.

"SCALAWAG, YOU'VE LOST YOUR SHIP AGAIN. BUT THIS TIME YOU WON'T BE LEFT ALL ALONE ON A DESERT PLANET. YOU'LL BE SPENDING PLENTY OF TIME WITH YOUR CREW—*IN PRISON*."

FIRST PUBLISHED IN THE UNITED STATES OF AMERICA IN 2007 BY WALKER PUBLISHING COMPANY, INC.
DISTRIBUTED TO THE TRADE BY HOLTZBRINCK PUBLISHERS

FOR INFORMATION ABOUT PERMISSION TO REPRODUCE SELECTIONS FROM THIS BOOK,
WRITE TO PERMISSIONS, WALKER & COMPANY, 104 FIFTH AVENUE, NEW YORK, NEW YORK 10011

LIBRARY OF CONGRESS CATALOGING-IN-PUBLICATION DATA
O'MALLEY, KEVIN.
CAPTAIN RAPTOR AND THE SPACE PIRATES / KEVIN O'MALLEY AND PATRICK O'BRIEN ;
ILLUSTRATIONS BY PATRICK O'BRIEN.
P.   CM.
SUMMARY: CAPTAIN RAPTOR AND THE CREW OF THE MEGATOOTH ARE CALLED BACK INTO
ACTION TO SAVE THE PLANET JURASSICA FROM ROGUE SPACE PIRATES.
ISBN-13: 978-0-8027-9571-7 • ISBN-10: 0-8027-9571-4 (HARDCOVER)
ISBN-13: 978-0-8027-9572-4 • ISBN-10: 0-8027-9572-2 (REINFORCED)
[1. DINOSAURS—FICTION. 2. PIRATES—FICTION. 3. SCIENCE FICTION.] I. O'BRIEN, PATRICK, ILL. II. TITLE.
PZ7.0526CSP 2007   [E]—DC22   2006101182

BOOK DESIGN BY PATRICK O'BRIEN
ART CREATED WITH WATERCOLOR AND GOUACHE
TYPESET IN ACTION MAN

VISIT WALKER & COMPANY'S WEB SITE AT WWW.WALKERYOUNGREADERS.COM

PRINTED IN CHINA
2 4 6 8 10 9 7 5 3 1 (HARDCOVER)
2 4 6 8 10 9 7 5 3 1 (REINFORCED)

ALL PAPERS USED BY WALKER & COMPANY ARE NATURAL, RECYCLABLE PRODUCTS MADE FROM
WOOD GROWN IN WELL-MANAGED FORESTS. THE MANUFACTURING PROCESSES CONFORM TO THE
ENVIRONMENTAL REGULATIONS OF THE COUNTRY OF ORIGIN.